The Amazing
Adventures of
DENNIS
THE MENACE

The Amazing Adventures of

DENNIS

THE MENACE

Based on the character created by Hank Ketcham

and adapted by Carl Memling from the television

scripts written by William Cowley, Peggy Chantler,

George Tibbles, Hannibal Coons and Milton Pascal

Illustrated by Lee Holley

Random House NEW YORK

MR. WILSON'S HELPER

It was a fine sunny morning. Birds made bright sounds above the lawn surrounding Dennis Mitchell's house.

"Oh, boy!" Dennis said. The pith helmet on his head bobbed up and down, and his eyes shone with excitement. "What a swell day for a lion hunt!"

His friend Tommy nodded happily. Holding up a ping-pong rifle, he said, "Kapow!"

Dennis said, "Look! There's the jungle!"

Tommy looked. But all he saw was a level stretch of lawn, then a gravel driveway glinting in the sunlight. And beyond that, a dense row of evergreen shrubs.

"Jungle?" Tommy said. "Where?"

"There! Those big green bushes! See them?"

Tommy stared and nodded.

Dennis caught his arm. "I go first," he said.

Dennis Mitchell, Big Game Hunter, moved swiftly off, followed by his Gun Bearer, Tommy Anderson. They reached the driveway, and gravel crunched underfoot. The "jungle" came closer and closer.

Suddenly Dennis froze. "Shhhh!" he warned.

Something stirred.

It could have been just a breeze. It could have been the push and rustle of a wild beast moving unseen through a jungle.

Dennis signalled for the rifle. Tommy thrust it at him.

Quickly Dennis raised it to his shoulder. Closing his eyes, he fired.

Pong! A ping-pong ball shot up into the air.

Flying swiftly, the white ball disappeared behind the evergreens. Then, just as swiftly, it came flying back and landed at their feet.

Tommy gulped and looked around. There was no one in sight. "Who threw it back?" Tommy whispered. "The lion?"

Before Dennis could answer, there came a sound of footsteps. A plump moon-faced man peered through the evergreens, then glared at them over the tops of his glasses.

The moment Dennis saw his elderly next-door neighbor, his face broke into a big smile. "Hi, Mr. Wilson," he said.

There was no answering smile on Mr. Wilson's face.

Dennis said, "Jeepers, Mr. Wilson, did I hit you? I was aiming at a lion."

"Did you see him, Mr. Wilson?" asked Tommy. "He was an awful big lion. And he was right in your part of the jungle."

Mr. Wilson took a long time answering. Finally he said, "No, I didn't! Nor have I seen any tigers, elephants, giraffes or baboons today. But I did see a ping-pong ball, which I tossed right back."

At this, Dennis's eyes went wide with awe. "Golly, Mr. Wilson," he said, "you sure are swell. You're the best friend I ever could have! Thanks a whole lot, Mr. Wilson."

Mr. Wilson looked dazed. "Thanks? For what, Dennis?"

"For telling us that there are no wild animals around. Now we can stop playing that dopey old game."

"Yeah," Tommy said. "That's right." But then he frowned. "Jeepers, Dennis, if we stop playing, we'll have nothing to do."

"We can always help good old Mr. Wilson," Dennis said. "Can't we, Mr. Wilson?"

Mr. Wilson glared. Turning, he marched stiffly to his dahlia bed. There he dropped to his knees and began to jab at the earth with a hand trowel.

"No, thank you, Dennis," he said in a cold voice.

"But isn't there anything we can do?" called Dennis.

"You could go home," Mr. Wilson suggested, but he didn't sound very hopeful.

Dennis called again. "Do you want to see how Tommy and I can climb your fence, Mr. Wilson?"

"I do not!" Mr. Wilson said.

"Okay," said Dennis. "We'll run around."

"No!" cried Mr. Wilson.

But it was too late. The front gate swung open, and Dennis and Tommy came dashing in.

With quick angry jabs, Mr. Wilson kept digging at the earth. The boys stood beside him, but their eyes wandered all over the garden. Over by the garage stood a wheelbarrow. It held what looked like a big black sand-pile of ground-up coffee beans.

"Boy," Dennis said, "that sure is a swell wheelbarrow."

"Yeah," Tommy said. "It sure is neat."

"You want us to move it closer to you?" asked Dennis.

"No," Mr. Wilson said in a hoarse voice. "Stay away from it. It's full of plant food."

There was a moment's silence.

Dennis said, "What time do you feed your plants, Mr. Wilson?"

"No special time," mumbled Mr. Wilson.

Tommy asked, "Do plants have teeth, Mr. Wilson?"

"Of course not!"

"But if plants don't have teeth, Mr. Wilson," said Dennis, "*how* do they eat their food?"

Mr. Wilson sat back on his heels. "Boys," he said wearily, "if I let you bring the wheelbarrow over here, will you both go home and let me work?"

Dennis beamed. "Sure, Mr. Wilson."

"And you'll make certain not to tip it over?"

"We won't spill it, Mr. Wilson," said Dennis. "Don't worry."

But Mr. Wilson did worry. He worried as the boys dashed across the garden. He worried as Dennis took one wooden handle and Tommy took the other. But he worried most as they staggered toward him, pushing the heavy wheelbarrow.

At last the wheelbarrow was near the dahlia bed. And not an ounce of plant food had spilled. Sighing with relief, Mr. Wilson turned back to his work.

When the boys set the wheelbarrow down behind him, Mr. Wilson didn't bother to turn around. He was that sure his worries were over.

"Thanks, boys," he said in a cheerful voice. "Goodby now."

"Don't you need some more help, Mr. Wilson?" Dennis asked.

Mr. Wilson snorted.

Dennis had promised to go home!

Rising to his feet, Mr. Wilson swung around. But the wheelbarrow was closer than he thought. He hit it with his hip. And, as it overturned, the wheelbarrow scattered plant food in all directions.

Tommy said, "Oooo."

For a second Mr. Wilson didn't move a hair. He just got red. Then he got white. Then he began to sputter. And he was just about to explode— when suddenly a cheerful voice said:

"Hello, Mr. Wilson. How are you today?"

DRUMMING UP A CUSTOMER

"If *some* young people would be less helpful," Mr. Wilson said in a hoarse voice, "I would feel much better."

The tall thin man standing at the front gate stared at the overturned wheelbarrow. "Boys will be boys," he said.

"Hi, Mr. Burnley," said Dennis. "Gee, I haven't seen you since you used to live here."

Mr. Burnley seemed surprised. "You remember me, do you, Dennis?"

"Sure I do," Dennis sang out. "I remember you from when Mrs. Burnley used to hang out the wash. She made you wear that long funny underwear."

Mr. Burnley coughed. "Children don't miss much, do they?" he said.

"They can drive you out of your mind," said Mr. Wilson. Then he shrugged. "But sometimes when I get to feeling sorry for myself, I just think of Dennis's mother. She deserves flowers every day in the week."

Dennis beamed and nodded.

Pointing to the empty house on the other side of his, Mr. Wilson asked, "Sold your house yet?"

"No," said Mr. Burnley with a sigh. "I may have to come down in my price a little."

"Oh, don't do that," said Mr. Wilson. "It's such a nice place. You shouldn't have any trouble getting your price."

Mr. Burnley's eyes brightened. "Look," he said, "if you can drum up a buyer for me, I'll gladly give you the five per cent commission."

Mr. Wilson hooked his thumb in his armpits. Sighing dreamily, he said, "Well, I haven't had much experience selling houses . . ."

"I'll help you drum up somebody, Mr. Wilson," Dennis offered.

Mr. Wilson glared. "Are you still here? Why don't you go home and talk to your mother?"

"Okay, Mr. Wilson," said Dennis. Then, as an afterthought, "Did you mean what you said about my Mom deserving flowers?"

"I most certainly did!" snorted Mr. Wilson, walking toward the front gate.

"Jeepers," Dennis said to Tommy, "isn't good old Mr. Wilson a swell friend! My Mom just loves flowers."

A few minutes later the back door of the Mitchell house swung open, then slammed shut with a bang as Dennis came dashing in.

"Look, Mom!" he cried. "I picked a whole bunch of flowers, just for you!"

"Oh, Dennis," Mrs. Mitchell exclaimed, "how sweet!"

But all through lunch Mrs. Mitchell was thoughtful. And finally she said, "Dennis, you didn't take the flowers from Mr. Wilson's yard, did you?"

Dennis nodded brightly. "Sure I did. Mr. Wilson says you deserve them every day in the week. . . . Say, Mom, have you see my drum any place?"

Next door Mr. Wilson was pacing back and forth in his living room. "Martha," he said, "I'll just have to do something about Dennis Mitchell."

Mrs. Wilson stood up. "Oh George, don't be so grumpy," she said. "Stretch out and have a nice nap while I go over to Helen Scott's."

Mr. Wilson lay down on the couch, and Mrs. Wilson placed a pillow under his head.

"Who's Helen Scott?" he asked sleepily.

"She's a very nice person I met at the bridge club. She's apartment hunting. And she asked me to come along for company."

"Have a good time, Martha," Mr. Wilson murmured.

Then he yawned and, closing his eyes, snuggled down on the pillow. In no time he was snoring peacefully.

Suddenly a dull boom thundered in the street.

Mr. Wilson gave a grunt and turned over on his side.

The booming did not stop. It grew louder and louder.

BABOOM, BABOOM, BABOOM.

"*House for sale!*" a voice called. "*House for sale!*"

Mr. Wilson sat up and looked about dazedly.

BABOOM! BABOOM! BABOOM!

"I don't believe it!" he muttered.

But now the voice was calling right outside his window. "HOUSE FOR SALE! HOUSE FOR SALE!"

17

Mr. Wilson nodded grimly. "I believe it," he said.

He ran over to the window and jerked it up. Poking his head out, he shouted, "Dennis Mitchell, stop pounding that drum!"

"Is something the matter, Mr. Wilson?" asked Dennis.

"I was trying to nap," replied Mr. Wilson in a choked voice.

"Oh," said Dennis. "*I* was trying to drum up a customer for Mr. Burnley's house."

A dark purple flush rose from Mr. Wilson's neck and flooded his face. With an angry snort, he slammed the window down.

Crash. The window pane splintered.

"That window sure breaks easy, doesn't it, Mr. Wilson?" said Dennis with a deep sigh. "Remember when my baseball went through it?"

Mr. Wilson remembered that very well. In fact, he was still remembering it when Mrs. Wilson returned.

"Martha," he said eagerly, "did you say the Scotts are looking for a new apartment?"

"That's right," replied Mrs. Wilson.

"Do they have any little children?"

"Of course not. They're our age."

"Good!" cried Mr. Wilson. He rubbed his hands together. "Keep your hat on, Martha. I'll get mine from the closet."

Mrs. Wilson looked puzzled. "Where are we going, George?"

"To the Scotts. I want to talk to them about buying a house!"

SURPRISE!

The sun was up bright and early next morning, and so was Mr. Wilson. For the first time in days, he whistled as he came down to breakfast.

"Good morning, Martha," he said in a loud cheery voice.

"Morning, George," said Mrs. Wilson.

"You didn't think I could do it, did you?" Mr. Wilson said with a chuckle. He paused to sip his orange juice. "Martha, you'll have to learn to have more faith in me."

Mrs. Wilson was silent for a while. Finally she said, "The Scotts may have agreed to look at the Burnley house this afternoon, but that doesn't mean they'll buy it."

"Martha," Mr. Wilson said, "there was a *reason* why I sold more auto parts than anyone else in this state. And that reason was salesmanship. When the Scotts hear my sales talk, they'll buy!"

Shortly after lunch the doorbell rang.

Chuckling, Mr. Wilson went to answer it.

"Hi, Mr. Wilson!"

"Dennis!" grumbled Mr. Wilson. "What are *you* doing here?"

"My dad sent me over to apologize. I'm sorry my drum woke you up yesterday."

"That's very nice of you, Dennis. Goodby now," said Mr. Wilson.

"And I sure am sorry that you broke your window, Mr. Wilson."

"That was my fault, Dennis. I shouldn't have lost my temper. Goodby now."

Dennis gave a deep sigh. "But if I can't use my drum, how can I help you sell Mr. Burnley's house?"

A terrible thought struck Mr. Wilson. "Dennis," he said in a small voice, "what are you going to be doing this afternoon?"

Dennis shrugged. "Jeepers, I don't know. Is there some game you want to play?"

"No!" Mr. Wilson said quickly.

He gave Dennis a very thoughtful look. Then he dug into his pocket and pulled out several coins. "Dennis," he said expansively, "here's fifty cents. Why don't you go see the movie down at the Arcade?"

Dennis's eyes almost popped out of his head. "Oh boy, thanks, Mr. Wilson. I'll go ask my mom."

"You do that," said Mr. Wilson. "And sit through the picture twice."

Mr. Wilson closed the door. And then he gave a wise smile. "That movie was a great idea," he told Mrs. Wilson. "If there's one thing that could ruin my sales talk to the Scotts, it's Dennis Mitchell."

Just then the doorbell rang again.

"Hi, Mr. Wilson," said Dennis. "Here's your fifty cents. I guess I can't go."

Mr. Wilson stood frozen on the threshold. "Why not?"

"Because when Tommy gets back from the dentist, he won't have any-body to play with."

Sighing heavily, Mr. Wilson dug into his pocket again. "Here's enough money so Tommy can go too," he said in a weak voice.

Mr. Wilson closed the door and leaned against it. "Whew!" he said. "That ends that. The next time that doorbell rings, I hope it will be our future neighbors coming to call."

But the next time the bell rang, it announced the arrival of a pleasant-faced young man in overalls who was carrying a tool kit.

"Mr. Wilson?" said the young man. "My name is Ferris. I've come to fix your broken window...."

Next door, Dennis dashed into his mother's kitchen and let out a joy-ous yell. "Mom, will it be okay if Tommy and I go to the…"

Suddenly Dennis's voice trailed off.

He sniffed, sighed, then sniffed again.

With eyes as wide as saucers, he stood and stared.

"I'm sorry, Dennis," said Mrs. Mitchell. She was spreading chocolate icing over a huge cake. "But this cake isn't for us. The McClures are having an anniversary and we're giving them a surprise party. The McClures don't know a thing about it. Tonight a lot of us will go to their house, and when they answer the door we'll all shout 'Surprise!' And then we'll rush in blowing horns and whistles."

"Say, that's neat!" cried Dennis. His face was all smiles. "I'll bring my bugle."

"I'm sorry, Dennis," said his mother. "This will be a party for grownups."

Dennis shrugged his shoulders and the smile faded from his face. "Well," he said in a low voice, "is it okay if Tommy and I go to the movies this afternoon?"

"I guess so," Mrs. Mitchell said. "Let me get my purse."

"You don't need to," said Dennis. "Good old Mr. Wilson is treating us."

With this, Dennis wheeled around and made a dash for the door. And by the time he reached Tommy's house, his face was all smiles again.

"It's all set," he told Tommy.

But Tommy's mother, Mrs. Anderson, said, "I'm sorry, Dennis. Tommy went to a movie with us just last night."

"But we have to do something!" Dennis wailed. "We've got all of Mr. Wilson's money to spend." Then, "I know what!" he said. "I'll buy a bunch of stuff to eat. And I'll give Tommy a surprise party."

But Mrs. Anderson was plainly horrified. "No," she said firmly. "Not in this house. I'm still finding traces of Tommy's last party."

"Okay," said Dennis. "Come on, Tommy. Let's see if we can give a surprise party in Freddy's house."

But Freddy's mother said no, too. So did Joey's mother. So did Stewart's. And so did Charley's, Philip's, and George's.

Dennis sat down on the curb to think. It was a big problem, all right. Where, where, oh where could they have the party?

A car came down the street. It stopped, and an elderly couple got out. Dennis watched them walk slowly along the path to Mr. Wilson's house.

Watching them gave Dennis an idea. He turned to his friends.

"Hey!" he said. "Why don't we give a surprise party for good old Mr. Wilson?"

There followed a very busy half-hour for Dennis and his friends.

On bikes, scooters, and roller skates, they all raced to the candy store. There they got a large container of chocolate ice cream—and as much bubble gum as the rest of Mr. Wilson's money would buy.

And then a Halloween costume in the window of the candy store gave Dennis another idea. Party costumes! All the kids had something at home they could dress up in.

When Dennis came out of his house a short time later, he was dressed in a monkey costume. The large container of chocolate ice cream was cradled in his left arm. With his right hand he held a bugle. On the way to Mr. Wilson's house, Dennis met a red devil carrying a trumpet, a pirate with a drum, a spaceman arm in arm with a skeleton, a jack o'lantern with a police whistle, and a tiger tuning up a harmonica....

Meanwhile, in his living room, Mr. Wilson was rubbing his hands together happily. After taking the Scotts on a tour of the Burnley house, he had brought them back here for coffee and the sales talk. And what a sales talk it had been!... Now that it was over, Mr. Wilson was breathless and the Scotts were spellbound.

The elderly couple sat perfectly still, with a faraway look in their eyes.

Mr. Ferris, the young man who had come to fix the window, was the first to break the silence.

"It sounds like a wonderful house," he said softly.

In a dazed voice, Mr. Scott said, "And the price is certainly right."

"And we like the neighborhood," Mrs. Scott added with a long sigh. "It's so quiet. And quiet is so important to us."

Mr. Wilson chuckled. "Well, that's that," he said. "I'll have Mr. Burnley get in touch with you."

At that moment the doorbell rang. And still chuckling, Mr. Wilson went to answer it. Then—a surprising thing happened. Right into Mr. Wilson's ear came a terrific blast of sound. He backed away, turning pale. Suddenly Mr. Wilson had no idea where he was. Rushing through the

open door came what appeared to be a small monkey. In one arm it held a large container. And it rushed around and around the room, blowing mighty blasts on a bugle.

Next Mr. Wilson thought he saw a red devil and a pirate come dashing in. At this he gave a strangled groan.

Suddenly a small spaceman whizzed by him, followed by a skeleton that skipped. Mr. Wilson tottered to the sofa and collapsed.

More horns blasted. From a harmonica came a shrill wail, and some-

body began beating a drum. Suddenly there was an ear-splitting whistle. "Surprise!" voices shouted. "Surprise...!"

With a heavy sigh, Mr. Wilson fainted dead away.

It took sometime before he was himself again.

"Martha," he called weakly. He lay stretched out on the couch, and Mrs. Wilson was bending over him. "What happened?"

"Dennis Mitchell gave a surprise party for you," replied Mrs. Wilson. "That was all."

Mr. Wilson stared up at her.

"George," said Mrs. Wilson, speaking very rapidly, "you should be proud. The Scotts just couldn't get over the way all those youngsters love you."

Mr. Wilson blinked his eyes and glanced about. "Where is everybody?"

"They went home," said Mrs. Wilson.

Then she went on to say, "By the way, about the Burnley house—the Scotts aren't going to buy it. After the party they decided this isn't such a quiet neighborhood after all."

Slowly Mr. Wilson sat up. With great effort he rose to his feet. He had a strange, wild look about him.

"George!" cried Mrs. Wilson. "Where are you going?"

"To bed," Mr. Wilson muttered. "I'm going to put my head under the covers. And when Dennis Mitchell comes calling, tell him I'm never coming out!"

FINCH'S DRUG STORE

The next few days passed very quickly.

Mr. Wilson came out again, of course. And Dennis Mitchell still called on him. But somehow Dennis couldn't spare as much time for Mr. Wilson as before. For one thing, he was busy saving up money for his mother's birthday.

One day Dennis was sitting on his bed. Beside him was an open piggy bank. He held two bills and some coins in his lap.

His friend Tommy asked, "How much do you have now, Dennis?"

"Two dollars...a nickel...and two pennies," Dennis said.

Tommy whistled. "Boy! That sure is a lot of money. How many birthday presents are you going to buy your mom?"

"Oh," said Dennnis with a shrug, "maybe fifty."

"Wow," Tommy said. Then, after a pause, "Where are you going to buy them all?"

"I don't know," said Dennis. "But that's okay. I bet good old Mr. Wilson knows a place."

Mr. Wilson was in his garden painting the rose trellis when the two boys arrived.

"Hi, Mr. Wilson," said Dennis.

The back of Mr. Wilson's neck turned bright red. Without turning around, he said, "Dennis, you may not *watch* me paint. And you may not *help* me paint. Now goodbye."

"Golly," Dennis said in a low voice. "I just came here because I have a problem."

Mr. Wilson put down his paint brush. Turning around, he asked suspiciously, "What kind of problem?"

"My mom's birthday is coming," Dennis explained, "and I'm going to buy her fifty presents."

The corners of Mr. Wilson's mouth twitched. "Well, that's fine," he said. "But what's the problem? Do you need money, is that it?"

"Nope," said Dennis, patting his pocket. "I have so much money I almost need a wallet. But I want to go to a good department store to buy the presents."

Mr. Wilson looked surprised. "There are lots of stores, Dennis. You know that."

"Sure, Mr. Wilson. Only I'm not allowed to cross the street."

"Hmm," said Mr. Wilson, stroking his chin. "That is a problem, isn't it?" After thinking for a moment, he said, "How about Finch's Drug Store? They have lots of things."

Dennis said, "Jeepers, thanks, Mr. Wilson. You're real smart."

Mr. Wilson cleared his throat. "Dennis," he said, "this is a very nice thing you're doing for your mother. Now when you get to the store, ask for Mr. Finch himself. He's a friend of mine, and he'll see to it that you get your money's worth."

"Okay, Mr. Wilson," said Dennis. "Goodbye!"

The boys dashed off with a leap and a yell. Mr. Wilson smiled fondly after them.

"Dennis is doing something very nice," Mr. Wilson said to himself. "And for once he's doing something that won't get me into any trouble."

That was what Mr. Wilson thought. But that is not what happened.

Dennis and Tommy dashed down the street. They ran up a driveway and climbed a fence. They dodged through a line full of clean wash hanging in a yard. Then they raced across an empty lot until they came to Finch's Drug Store.

The store was large and very cluttered. It had many counters, all of them piled high with different things.

The boys paused, speechless with delight. Their eyes shone.

An icy voice said, "Well, what do you want?"

Startled, they looked up to see a man fussing with some bottles at a counter. The man wore a smock, and he had a cross and peevish expression on his face.

Dennis squared his shoulders. "I want to buy fifty presents for my mom, for her birthday."

"Fifty?" sneered the man, who was Mr. Finch. "Do you have any money?"

Dennis patted his pocket. "I've got loads of money."

"He got it out of his bank...dollar bills and everything," Tommy added.

"Bank, eh?" Suddenly Mr. Finch seemed very friendly. Leaning forward on the counter, he said, "What exactly did you have in mind, son?"

"Are you Mr. Finch?" Dennis wanted to know. "I have to get all the presents from a Mr. Finch, because he's a friend of Mr. Wilson's."

"Wilson?" said Mr. Finch. "George Wilson?"

Dennis nodded.

"Well, why didn't you say so before? George Wilson is a friend of mine. So *he* sent you to me?...How nice of him!"

Rubbing his hands together, Mr. Finch went on smoothly, "Why don't you walk around the store, son? Take a good look."

"Okay," said Dennis.

As the boys walked off, a dreamy look came over Mr. Finch's face. He was already adding up prices in his mind. Fifty presents...at so much a present...came to quite a sum of money!

The boys walked along the aisles until they came to a huge pile of things on the floor.

Dennis stopped. He tilted his head back and his eyes widened. In the pile were basketballs in boxes, rubber swim fins, underwater goggles, ping-pong paddles—and even three blown-up plastic wading pools.

"I think I'll get my mom a wading pool and some swim fins," Dennis said.

"Your mother likes the water, does she?" asked Mr. Finch, coming up behind him.

Dennis nodded. "Boy, I'll say! She takes a bath every day."

Then Dennis noticed a huge rubber raft pressed flat at the bottom of the pile. Next to it was a sign with the words SELF-INFLATING LIFE RAFT—ANNUAL SPECIAL.

"And I think I'll get her one of those, too," Dennis said.

Mr. Finch took an order book out of his pocket and started writing slowly and with great pleasure:

> *One pair of swim fins*
> *One inflatable rubber life raft*

Tommy frowned at the deflated raft. "It doesn't even look as if it would float," he said.

"Maybe you have to put air in it," said Dennis. "You know, same as a tire." With these words, he began to inspect the raft. Finding a rubber plug, Dennis gave it a pull.

At once there was a hiss of air.

"Boy," said Dennis, "look at that old raft swell up."

"Oh, no!" cried Mr. Finch, glancing up from his order book.

Panic-stricken, he kneeled and fumbled with the rubber plug. But air kept hissing and the raft kept swelling. It began to shift and move about, as if alive.

Hssss...

Now the whole pile of things above the swelling raft began to totter. A wading pool slid slowly down. With a soft thump, it landed on top of Mr. Finch.

Thump, thump. Two more wading pools came sliding down.

Swim fins came flopping. Ping-pong paddles clattered. Boxes thudded to the floor. They burst open, and basketballs bounced along the aisles.

Hssss...

The swelling raft moved about some more. Suddenly tilting up, it floated against a counter.

Crash! Sixteen jumbo-sized bottles of shampoo fell and broke into a thousand pieces.

Dennis slowly shook his head from side to side. "I don't think I want that raft any more," he said. "It's getting too fat."

"Help!" Mr. Finch's voice called weakly. "Get me out of here!"

It was Dennis who finally pulled the last pool off Mr. Finch's head.

But instead of thanking Dennis, the proprietor shouted, "Just wait till I get that George Wilson for sending such a store wrecker to me!"

Dennis stared at him, bewildered.

"Just you wait, George Wilson!" Mr. Finch added in his grimmest voice. "Just...you...wait!"

THE SIGNPOST

At breakfast next morning Dennis's father was not in his best mood. Drinking his coffee in quick gulps, he said, "Dennis, you'll just have to learn to leave Mr. Wilson alone."

"Jeepers," said Dennis. "I only asked him for the name of a good department store. That's all I did yesterday."

Mr. Mitchell's eyebrows went up. "That's all? Do you know what happened? Mr. Finch called Mr. Wilson up on the phone. Mr. Finch was fit to be tied. It took almost all night before Mr. Wilson could calm his old friend down."

"Dear," said Dennis's mother quickly, "have another piece of toast."

Dennis slowly spooned his cereal. He could tell from his father's tone of voice that Mr. Mitchell was really cross.

"Golly," Dennis thought to himself. "I never even got one present for Mom yesterday. I should be cross, too."

"Dennis," his father went on sternly, "you're not to step inside Mr. Wilson's yard all day today. Do you understand?"

Dennis hung his head. "Yes, Dad."

His mother looked troubled. "Dear," she said to Mr. Mitchell, "Dennis didn't mean any harm..."

That was exactly what Mrs. Wilson was saying next door at that moment:

"Dear...Dennis didn't mean any harm."

Mr. Wilson gave a loud groan. "Dennis never does," he said. "It's just that he's such a jinx. Every time he shows up, terrible things happen."

Mr. Wilson groaned all through breakfast. With his coffee, he took a big dose of nerve medicine.

After breakfast he walked into the living room—and Mrs. Wilson stared at what he was carrying. He had a hammer, a ball of string, and about a dozen wooden pegs.

"Are you feeling any better, dear?" Mrs. Wilson asked.

Slowly Mr. Wilson laid down the hammer, string, and all the wooden pegs. "A little. Thank you, Martha," he groaned, reaching for the telephone.

"Oh, George," said Mrs. Wilson. "Can't you let bygones be bygones? Henry Mitchell promised to keep Dennis away. Why call him again?"

Dialing, Mr. Wilson said, "I happen to be calling a garden nursery."

Mrs. Wilson was silent for a while. Finally she said, "I thought you were going to reseed the backyard yourself."

"So did I!" Mr. Wilson said with an angry snort. "But after everything that's happened to me lately, I'm just not up to it." A stricken look came over his face. "Thanks to Dennis, I lost the commission on the Burnley house. I almost lost an old friend. And now I have to lay out over a hundred dollars to have the back lawn reseeded."

By now Mr. Wilson had the garden nursery on the phone.

"Hello. This is George Wilson of 625 Elm Street," he said. "I'd like a reseeding job done on my back lawn. No, not the whole lawn, just part of it. Could you send some men over tomorrow?...You could? Fine!... No, I won't be home..."

At this, Mrs. Wilson lifted her head and gave a puzzled frown.

"Yes, the part I want reseeded will be all staked out," continued Mr. Wilson. "As a matter of fact, I'm just about to do it now. When your men come, they can go right to work. Just make sure you have the right address. 625 Elm Street...."

At last Mr. Wilson hung up. Before he could turn around, Mrs. Wilson said in a puzzled voice, "George?"

"Yes, Martha?"

"Why did you tell the garden nursery you wouldn't be here tomorrow?"

"Because I *won't* be," said Mr. Wilson firmly. "Martha, I want the two of us to get away tomorrow. From Dennis Mitchell. We'll hit that open road and we'll take a nice long ride in the country."

Sighing dreamily, Mr. Wilson picked up the hammer, string, and all the wooden pegs. "Now while *you* plan tomorrow's picnic basket, Martha," he said with a smile, "*I'll* go out to stake the lawn for reseeding."

A short time later Dennis came out of his house and heard the sound of hammering. He stopped and listened. The hammering was coming from Mr. Wilson's yard.

What was good old Mr. Wilson building now? Dennis wondered.

Peering through the pickets of the fence, he saw Mr. Wilson driving wooden pegs into the ground.

Soon Mr. Wilson had hammered in enough pegs to stake out an area fifteen feet by twenty-five feet. Now he reached for the ball of string. Knotting the end of the string, he tied it to a peg. Then he pulled the string taut. But just as he was going to tie it to the next peg, he heard a familiar voice.

"What are you doing, Mr. Wilson?" Dennis called from the fence.

Mr. Wilson said in a dull voice, "I'm tying strings to the pegs."

There was a long silence.

Finally Dennis called, "Why are you tying up those pegs?"

Mr. Wilson pressed his lips together. "I'm not going to tell you."

"But if you don't tell me what you're doing, *how* can I ever help you?"

"You can't!" Mr. Wilson said with a snort. "And stop trying."

A bewildered look came over Dennis's face. "But *why*, Mr. Wilson?

After all—friends *always* help their friends."

Mr. Wilson glanced down at his hands. They were shaking. "Dennis," he said hoarsely, "go away!"

Poor Mr. Wilson! Dennis sighed deeply. "You want me to get some nerve medicine for you?" he asked.

"No! Just go away!"

"Okay," said Dennis. And he went away.

But as he went, he wondered about all those pegs Mr. Wilson had banged into the ground. Why wouldn't Mr. Wilson tell what they were for? Whatever it was, it sure was going to be something awfully big!

Dennis frowned. Secrets! Why did grownups always have to have so many secrets! That must be why Mr. Wilson was so nervous today.

"Jeepers!" thought Dennis. "When *I* grow up, I'll never keep any secrets from my..." But Dennis never got to finish his thought, for just

then he reached the front sidewalk and almost ran into Tommy.

"Hi," said Tommy. "How's Mr. Wilson?"

"He's swell," said Dennis. "He's up already and building something secret in his yard. Its going to be something awfully big."

The two boys walked along Elm Street, kicking stones. Soon they were near the corner.

"Hey, look!" Dennis yelled suddenly.

Looking up, Tommy saw a station wagon driving off. And then he saw the signpost at the corner of Elm and Mississippi streets.

It was lying on the grass strip next to the curb. Near it was the hole in which it had stood. The wooden arm that said *Elm* was flat on the ground. The arm that said *Mississippi* was pointed toward an airplane buzzing slowly across the sky.

"You see what happened there?" Dennis said. "That car just knocked down the sign. *Kapow!*"

"Yeah," said Tommy excitedly. "*Kapow!*"

Dennis said in a serious voice, "With a knocked down signpost, the ice cream man could get lost. We'd better put it up again."

Pulling and pushing with all their strength, the two boys heaved the signpost back into its hole. Then, while Dennis held it straight, Tommy stamped with his feet all around the base. Finally Dennis let go. And the pole wasn't wobbly any more.

"Now nobody will get lost," said Dennis with a smile.

Beaming, Tommy said, "Yeah. Now we can go home and wait for the ice cream man."

Glowing with pride, the boys walked away.

Behind them the signpost stood erect.

But now the arm that said *Elm* pointed to Mississippi Street. And the arm that said *Mississippi* pointed to Elm Street.

THE ENORMOUS HOLE

The next day dawned warm and clear. It was perfect weather for a ride in the country. And Mr. Wilson was in excellent spirits.

"Come on, Martha!" he called. "Let's hit that open road!"

Mrs. Wilson came to the front door carrying a picnic basket. "George, don't forget to put up the note for the seed men," she said.

"I almost did forget," said Mr. Wilson with a frown. He shook his head. "I guess I'm just so anxious to get away before Dennis sees us."

Rushing inside, Mr. Wilson quickly wrote a note. It said:

I'll be away for the day. The yard is all staked out—
you can go right in.

As he taped the note to the outside of the front door, his hands trembled with joy.

With a courtly bow, Mr. Wilson held the car door open for his wife. As she stepped in, he chuckled happily.

"Helloooooo, Mr. Wilson!" a voice sang out.

"Where are you going, Mr. Wilson?" asked Dennis, rushing to the curb.

"Dennis, we're going for a ride in the country," answered Mrs. Wilson for her husband.

As Mr. Wilson slid stiffly into the driver's seat, Dennis peeked into the car. "Ooooow," he said with eyes wide as saucers. "I see a big picnic basket in there. Do you want *me* to come with you?"

Suddenly a thought struck Mr. Wilson. A clever smile stole over his face. Dennis was always trying to help him! If he gave Dennis a job to do now, Dennis would forget all about going on the picnic.

Mr. Wilson chuckled, rubbed his hands together, and winked broadly at his wife.

Then, forcing himself to look serious, he said in a grave voice, "Dennis, I'd like to have you come with us. But there's an important job for you to do here."

Dennis could hardly believe his ears. Mr. Wilson was asking *him* for help!

"Some men are coming by in a truck to do some work in my back yard," said Mr. Wilson, still speaking in a grave voice. "When they get here, will you tell them to go right to work?"

"I sure will," said Dennis eagerly

Mr. Wilson chuckled. "I knew you'd do it," he said. "After all, don't friends *always* help their friends?"

With these words, the Wilsons drove off.

Mrs. Wilson smiled as she waved goodby to Dennis. She was still smiling as the car sped by the signpost at the corner.

Dennis watched the car grow smaller and smaller. At last it made a turn, and the street was empty.

Dennis stood perfectly still. He could hear his heart pounding. Good old Mr. Wilson had nothing to worry about! He had given an important job to the right boy!

An hour later Dennis was still standing in front of Mr. Wilson's house. But now he was shaking his head gravely.

"Nope," he said to Tommy. "I can't have a race with you today. Can't you see I'm doing an important job for Mr. Wilson?"

Tommy and Stewart looked puzzled. They were on their scooters.

"What job?" Tommy wanted to know.

Stewart said, "You're just standing there not doing anything."

Just then a big truck stopped at the corner. The truck was hauling a bulldozer on a flat open trailer. The truckdriver stuck his head out and looked at the signpost. Then he looked at a slip of paper in his hand.

"We're here," he said to his helper. "This is Mississippi Street. 625 must be right down that way."

"We're lucky we saw this signpost," said the helper. "Otherwise, we might have gone down Elm Street by mistake."

The big truck moved slowly along the street.

Dennis gave a sudden jump. *"Hallllooooo, there!"* he yelled. *"Here it is! This is the house!"*

The driver stopped. He stuck his head out and looked at the number of Mr. Wilson's house. It was 625. Then he looked at the number on the slip of paper in his hand. It was 625.

"This looks like the place, all right," he said to his helper. Then he called down, "Anybody home?"

"No," Dennis called back. "But they told me to tell you to go right to work in the back yard."

"Okay," called the driver. Then he said to his helper, "I see a note on the front door. You better go see what it says."

The helper stepped down from the truck and walked up the path to Mr. Wilson's house. At the door he read the note which said:

I'll be away for the day. The yard is all staked out—you can go right in.

Nodding, the helper crumpled up the note and put it in his pocket. Then he walked around the house to take a look at the yard.

"You want me to help you steer the truck in?" Dennis asked the waiting driver.

Just then the helper came back. "The yard is all staked out with pegs," he said. "I guess we can start right in."

"Okay," said the driver, swinging himself down off the truck.

Dennis stiffened. Pegs!

Now he was going to find out Mr. Wilson's secret!

Pointing to the yard, Dennis asked, "What are you going to do there?"

"Don't you know?" said the driver. "We're going to put in a swimming pool."

The driver and his helper got to work at once.

In scarcely any time at all, they had the bulldozer down off the trailer and in Mr. Wilson's back yard. There the driver quickly steered over to where the grass was staked out, and pulled a lever.

Clawing at Mr. Wilson's lawn, the bulldozer scooped out a bucketload of earth. The driver yanked another lever, and the bucket swung slowly up and over to the side. The driver yanked again. This time the load slid

out in a cloud of dust. And then the bucket swung back to claw at Mr. Wilson's lawn again.

This happened over and over again.

Soon there was an enormous hole in Mr. Wilson's lawn.

The driver kept yanking. The bucket kept clawing. The hole in Mr. Wilson's lawn grew more and more enormous. And Dennis and his friends grew more and more excited.

As fast as legs and scooters could carry them, they spread the news. Up and down Elm Street, they rang every doorbell. They shouted the news to all the neighbors, old and young.

One lady said, "I'm glad you told me, Dennis. I simply wouldn't have believed it."

"Oh, I've been telling everybody," said Dennis, dashing off. "Good old Mr. Wilson is going to have a swimming pool, all right."

Soon all the grownups on Elm Street knew what was going on in Mr. Wilson's yard. And some of them dropped by to take a look.

They watched the bulldozer at work. They saw the size of the enormous hole. And their eyes went wide with wonder.

"Imagine Mr. Wilson keeping this a secret all the time!" one woman said.

Meanwhile the driver kept yanking. The bucket kept clawing. And the hole in Mr. Wilson's lawn grew more and more enormous.

Suddenly the driver pressed a button—and the dozer stopped.

"Let's rest up a while," he said. "I'm worn out."

"So am I," said his helper. "This is a big job."

The driver took a pack of cigarettes from his pocket and stuck one in his mouth. Lighting up, he said, "By the time we're finished, this hole will be plenty big."

"Hey!" cried Dennis. "You want me to drive the bulldogger for awhile?"

"Bulldozer—not bulldogger," said the driver with a smile. "No, thanks."

The men got back to work. And it was almost evening when they finished. Yawning tiredly, the driver and his helper loaded the dozer back on the trailer. As they drove off, Dennis waved goodby to them.

And then Dennis went back to see the enormous hole again. He stared down at it for a long while. "Know what?" Dennis said to himself. "When Mr. Wilson sees this hole tonight, nobody will have to tell him what a neat job I did!"

But it was very dark when the Wilsons came home that night.

Tired but happy, they got out of the car.

"It's been a nice day, George," said Mrs. Wilson.

Mr. Wilson nodded. "Very nice, Martha. Perfect."

"Do you want to go into the yard to look at the seeding job?"

Mr. Wilson smiled sleepily. "Thank you, Martha. It's very thoughtful of you to remind me." Then he yawned. "But it's too dark now to see anything. I'll look tomorrow."

AIR RAID!

Morning came to Elm Street.

Everything was very peaceful.

Mr. Wilson's eyes blinked slowly open and he stared for a while at the clock beside his bed.

"Martha," he said finally, "we've overslept."

"Have we?" murmured Mrs. Wilson.

Mr. Wilson smiled at a shaft of sunlight slanting in through the window on the other side of the bedroom. "And it's a wonderful, wonderful day!" he said in a soft voice.

Mrs. Wilson stared at him. "Well," she said, "you *are* in a good mood this morning."

Mr. Wilson gave a gentle chuckle. "Why shouldn't I be?" he wanted to know. "That drive in the country was a great tonic for my nerves."

"Was it really? I'm glad, George."

"Yes, Martha," said Mr. Wilson. "I feel so peaceful. I've never felt this way before. I'm like a new man."

Mr. Wilson paused. A moment later a tear of joy came to his eye. "I wonder where Dennis Mitchell is right now," he said. "My, but he's a nice, clean-cut youngster . . ."

Dennis was out in the street with Tommy.

Tommy was holding a giant firecracker. And Dennis was staring at it.

Dennis gulped. The firecracker was only slightly smaller than a rolling pin.

"Wow!" said Dennis. "That's the biggest firecracker I *ever* saw. Where'd you find it?"

"In my attic," said Tommy.

"Wow!" repeated Dennis. "You better give it to me, because firecrackers are dangerous."

Tommy pouted. But then he handed over the giant firecracker.

"I'll take it over to my house and throw it away," said Dennis.

Slowly Tommy followed him into Mrs. Mitchell's kitchen. There Dennis stuck the giant firecracker into a bag of trash on the sink.

Turning away, Dennis said, "Now nobody will get hurt."

"Let's go look at the big hole in Mr. Wilson's yard," Tommy said.

"We can't," said Dennis. "On account of the Wilsons are still sleeping. And my dad won't let us go."

Tommy gave a heavy sigh. "Jeepers, there's nothing to do."

A thought struck Dennis. "Hey, Tommy," he said, "you want to go to Stewart's house?"

"Okay," said Tommy. And he followed Dennis out.

Dennis's father almost followed him out, too.

Mr. Mitchell had his hat on. He had just said goodby to Mrs. Mitchell, and he had just picked up his briefcase.

"Dear," called Mrs. Mitchell, "will you take this out to the incinerator for me?"

By "this," Mrs. Mitchell meant the bag of trash that had been standing on the kitchen sink.

"Be glad to, dear," replied Mr. Mitchell.

With these words, he put down his briefcase and took the trash bag.

As Mr. Mitchell carried the bag toward the incinerator, he whistled a happy tune.

Dennis's father would have whistled a quite different tune if he had known that there was a firecracker in the bag—and that the firecracker was only slightly smaller than a rolling pin!

Meanwhile, Mr. Wilson was still in a wonderful mood. Propped against his pillow, he sat up in bed with his fingers laced behind his neck.

Sighing happily, he said, "You'll see, Martha. I'm going to be a different man from now on. No more scolding when Dennis drops by. You know, deep down inside I'm very fond of Dennis. And from now on I want to show it. Martha, why don't you make some cookies . . ."

Just then something exploded with a thunderous blast.

Springing out of bed, Mr. Wilson cried, "Great Scott! What was that!"

Trembling, Mrs. Wilson put her hand to her mouth. "George—it—it sounded like a bomb."

Mr. Wilson rushed over to the window.

He took a look and his face turned pale.

Mr. Wilson felt weak. He brushed his hand across his eyes and looked harder. "*Martha!*" he stammered. "C-c-come here!"

Dragging her feet, Mrs. Wilson forced herself to join him at the window. There she took a look and her eyes bulged.

"George," she whispered, staring down at the enormous hole in their back yard, "what could it be?"

"Martha," said Mr. Wilson, trying to keep his voice steady, "it's a bomb crater!"

"George! What'll we do!"

For a moment Mr. Wilson said nothing, but his jaw firmed. Then, reaching for his bathrobe, he said in a grave voice, "I must do my duty. You get under the bed."

Grimly Mr. Wilson pulled on his robe. Reaching into the closet, he pulled out an air raid warden's helmet and clapped it on his head.

"George!" moaned Mrs. Wilson. "Be careful!"

"Careful?" said Mr. Wilson in a scornful voice. "When my country is being attacked?"

And he ran out into the street yelling at the top of his lungs, "Air raid! Air raid! Everybody get to your shelters!"

THE BEST OF FRIENDS

"Air raid!" Mr. Wilson yelled, dashing up and down Elm Street. "Take cover, everybody!"

Doors opened all along the street. Men, women, and children peered out, their eyes wide with astonishment.

"To the shelters!" Mr. Wilson yelled. "Everybody to the shelters!"

One woman shook her head sadly. "Poor Mr. Wilson's mind has snapped," she said.

Another woman said, "He always was a very nervous man."

A third said, "What a pity! Now he'll never get to enjoy his lovely swimming pool."

All this while Dennis's father was standing by the incinerator in his own back yard. Mr. Mitchell's face and clothing were all covered with soot. And he was slightly dazed.

What could have been in that bag of trash? . . . One moment, whistling a happy tune, he had tossed it into the incinerator. The next moment it had exploded with a thunderous blast.

Mr. Mitchell frowned, puzzled.

Just then he heard a voice yelling, "Air raid! Air raid!"

Rushing up front, he came face to face with Mr. Wilson.

He stared at the air raid warden's helmet on Mr. Wilson's head.

Mr. Wilson stared at the soot all over Mr. Mitchell's face and clothing.

"Great Scott!" Mr. Wilson cried. "Our first casualty!"

"What!" gasped Mr. Mitchell.

"Take cover, Henry," said Mr. Wilson in a grave voice. "I'll call a medic for you as soon as I've alerted the others."

But before he could dash off again, Dennis's father grabbed him and held him firmly. "Wilson, what's going on?" he wanted to know.

"We're being bombed!" cried Mr. Wilson. "There's a bomb crater in my back yard!"

"Bomb crater? . . . *That's* the hole for your swimming pool!"

Mr. Wilson's mouth went slack with shock.

"Swimming pool?" he said in a dazed voice. "What are you talking about?" Slowly he shook his head. "I don't have any swimming pool . . ."

"Sure you have, Mr. Wilson," said Dennis, who had come running up. "Don't you remember my important job? *I* showed the men where to dig it."

Mr. Wilson shut his eyes tight, then opened them.

"Please, Henry," he said brokenly to Dennis's father, "take me home . . ."

Mr. Mitchell said sternly, "Wait right here, Dennis. When I come out, I'll have a great deal to say to you."

Dennis and Tommy sat on the curb, waiting gloomily.

"Boy, Dennis, your dad sure sounded angry," Tommy said.

Dennis winced. "Yeah . . . he sure did."

There was a long silence.

Time passed slowly.

"Dennis," said a voice.

The boys whirled around.

Mr. Wilson was standing on the grass strip right behind them. He looked very glum. Next to him stood Dennis's father.

"Dennis," his father said in a stern voice, "there's been quite a mix-up . . ."

"The swimming pool company just phoned me," Mr. Wilson said gloomily. "It seems that the signpost at the corner was turned the wrong way. So instead of digging a pool at 625 *Mississippi*, they came here to *Elm* Street."

His father scowled. "They never had a chance to find out their mistake, Dennis. *You* put them right to work."

Dennis gulped.

"But they're being very nice about it," his father went on.

"Yes," Mr. Wilson said gloomily. "They're going to fill in the hole, bring in new topsoil, and reseed—all at their expense. I'm really very lucky."

Dennis stared.

Why was Mr. Wilson so sad—if he was so very lucky?

"Dennis," his father said, "the next time Mr. Wilson might not be so lucky. You understand that, don't you?"

"Please, Dennis, don't ever try to help me again," Mr. Wilson was about to say. But just then a car pulled up. And out hopped Mr. Burnley.

Grasping Mr. Wilson's hand, he pumped it hard.

"You don't know how much I appreciate what you've done for me, Mr. Wilson," he said. "What a sales talk you must have given! Young Ferris still can't get it out of his mind. He called me at my office today."

"Y-you mean that the young man who came to fix my window bought your house?" Mr. Wilson stammered.

"That's right. And all on the strength of your sales talk," Mr. Burnley said with a smile. "I'm very grateful. Yes, sir. It'll really be a pleasure paying you a five percent commission."

Mr. Wilson blinked his eyes and scratched his head. He looked as if he couldn't believe his ears.

But then he gave a cry of triumph. "I *knew* that was a great sales talk!"

Mr. Wilson began to snicker.

Then he chuckled.

"Are you my friend again?" Dennis asked.

"Am I?" cried Mr. Wilson. "Why, Dennis, we're the best of friends! If not for you Mr. Ferris would never have come to fix the window. . . . If not for you, I'd never have gotten a free re-seeding job!"

Dennis beamed.

Mr. Wilson laughed and then he roared.

"Dennis, dear friend," he panted, "you've done so much for me. Is there anything I can do for you today?" Bending down, he added, "just name it, Dennis—and I'll do it."

So, cupping his hand to Mr. Wilson's ear, Dennis named it in a whisper. *"Take me back to Mr. Finch's so I can get the presents for my mom."*

And then Dennis stared, bewildered.

Why wasn't good old Mr. Wilson laughing any more . . . ?